MARTINEZ KIDS ADVENTURES

THE SECRET DOOR

Books open the door of your imagination! Minda Gomez

Written and illustrated by

Minda Gomez

For Rafa, Dante, and Amalia,
my three little adventurers.

Para mi amor, Moisés.
Gracias por siempre apoyarme en mis sueños.

Layout and Design by Moisés Gómez, MoGo Multimedia
Revision and editing by Judy Johnson

First paperback edition 2021
ISBN 978-0-578-97215-2

Table of Contents

Spanish Word Glossary

Part 1: Treetop Adventure
Value: Contentment
Chapter 1: Breakfast Tacos
Chapter 2: The Door
Chapter 3: Into the Trees
Chapter 4: Coco

Part 2: Ocean Adventure
Value: Honesty
Chapter 1: The Secret Mission
Chapter 2: Tortillas de Harina
Chapter 3: Swimming Lessons
Chapter 4: The Undersea Heist
Chapter 5: The Pearl

Part 3: Rainforest Adventure
Value: Wisdom
Chapter 1: The Dare
Chapter 2: The Ninja Park
Chapter 3: Rainforest Antics
Chapter 4: The Jungle Castle

Recipe: Mami's Spicy Turkey Quesadillas

About the Author

NAMES

Name	Pronunciation
Martinez	mar-TEE-nes
Rico	REE-co
Diego	dee-AY-go
Dieguito	dee-ay-GEE-to
Araceli	a-ra-SELL-ee
Mami	MAH-mee
Papi	PAH-pee
Don	DOHN
Doña	DOHN-yah
Toño	TOHN-yo
Rosa	RO-sah

SPANISH WORDS

Spanish	English	Pronunciation
A comer	Time to eat	(AH co-MAIR)
Amiguitos	Little friends	(ah-mee-GEE-toce)
Amores	My loves	(ah-MORE-ace)
Ándale	Get going	(AHN-dah-lay)
Ándale, pues	OK, go ahead	(AHN-dah-lay PWAYCE)
Ardillas	Squirrels	(ar-DEE-yahs)
Bendecidos	Blessed	(ben-deh-SEE-doce)
Bien	Well	(bee-EN)
Bienvenidos	Welcome	(bee-en-ven-EE-doce)
Buenas tardes	Good afternoon	(BWAY-nahs TAHR-dayce)
Bueno…	Well...	(BWAY-no)
Buenos días	Good morning	(BWAY-nos DEE-us)
Carne asada	Grilled meat	(CAR-nay ah-SAH-dah)
Casa	House	(CAH-sah)
Chamacos	Kids	(chah-MAH-koce)
Chicos	Boys	(CHEE-koce)
Chido	Cool	(CHEE-doh)
Chiles rellenos	Stuffed peppers	(CHEE-lace ray-YAY-nos)
Chupacabras	A mythical creature said to live in Mexico	(choo-pah-CAH-brus)
Claro que sí	Of course	(CLAH-row KAY SEE)
Coco	Coconut	(COE-coe)
Colibrí	Hummingbird	(coe-lee-BREE)
Comál	Griddle	(co-MAL)
¿Cómo estás?	How are you?	(CO-mo eh-STAHS)
Delicioso	Delicious	(day-lee-see-OH-so)
Don	Mr.	(DOHN)
Doña	Mrs.	(DO-nya)

SPANISH WORDS

Spanish	English	Pronunciation
Enchiladas	Rolled tortillas filled with meat, cheese, and salsa	(en-chee-LAH-dus)
¿Es cierto?	Is that true?	(ES see-AIR-to)
Es un placer	It's a pleasure	(es UN plah-SARE)
Fabuloso	Fabulous	(fah-boo-LOE-soe)
Gracias	Thank you	(GRA-see-us)
Hasta pronto	See you soon	(AH-stah PRON-toe)
Hermana	Sister	(air-MAH-nah)
Hermano	Brother	(air-MAH-no)
Hijo	Son	(EE-ho)
Hijos	Children	(EE-hoce)
Hola	Hello	(OH-lah)
La práctica hace el maestro	Practice makes perfect	(LAH PRAC-tee-cah AH-say EL my-AY-stro)
Las Pozas	The Pools (an artistic castle built near Xilitla, San Luis Potosi, Mexico)	(LAHS POH-sus)
Mi amor	My love	(MEE ah-MORE)
Mi vida	My life (term of affection)	(MEE VEE-dah)
Mi´jo (mi hijo)	My son	(MEE-ho)
Mis amigos	My friends	(MEES ah-MEE-goce)
Muchacho	Boy	(moo-CHAH-cho)
Muchas gracias	Thank you very much	(MOO-chus GRAH-see-us)
Niños	Kids	(NEE-nyoce)
¡Órale!	Wow!	(OH-rah-lay)
Pan dulce	Sweet bread	(PAHN DOOL-say)

SPANISH WORDS

Spanish	English	Pronunciation
Perla	Pearl	(PAIR-lah)
Pozole	Soup with meat and hominy (corn)	(po-SO-lay)
Preciosa	Precious	(pre-see-OH-sah)
¿Qué onda contigo?	What's going on with you?	(kay OHN-da cohn-TEE-go)
Quesadilla	Quesadilla	kay-sah-DEE-ya
Siesta	Nap	(see-ES-tah)
Te amo	I love you	(tay AH-mo)
Tortillas de harina	Flour tortillas	(tor-TEE-us DAY a-REE-nah)
¡Vámonos, pues!	Let's go!	(VAH-mo-noce PWACE)
Vamos	Let's go	(VAH-moce)
¡Ya voy!	I'm coming!	(YAH VOY)

Part 1

THE TREETOP ADVENTURE

Chapter 1
Breakfast Tacos

It was a typical morning in the Martinez *casa.* Shouts rang out through the house as Rico and Diego raced each other to the bathroom to wash their hands. Little Araceli pattered behind and jumped up on the step stool after her brothers left, splashing water everywhere in the process. The three children settled into their seats at the kitchen table and waited impatiently for their breakfast to be served.

Papi scooped steaming eggs scrambled with onions and peppers from the frying pan onto each child's plate. He placed warm corn tortillas on the table, along with their family's favorite guacamole salsa. He was happy to be able to make such a nutritious and tasty Mexican breakfast for his family.

Before he was even able to sit down himself, the complaining started. "Eggs again?!" grumbled Rico, who at eight years of age, was the oldest of the three. "Why don't we ever have anything GOOD for breakfast? I want something I can put syrup on."

Five-year-old Diego, always quick to follow his older brother, agreed. "I want to eat pancakes today."

Their two-year-old sister Araceli repeated, "Pancakes!"

Papi sighed. *"Hijos,* you will eat what I put in front of you," he said firmly, then turned to pour milk into his children's cups. As he placed them in front of the kids, he braced himself for what he knew was coming next.

"Milk again?! Why can't we drink juice for breakfast? My friends at school have juice and pancakes EVERY day for breakfast!" whined Rico.

"Yeah, I'm sick of milk and eggs!" complained Diego.

"Me too!" agreed Araceli, pushing her plate away.

Mami entered the kitchen, overhearing the conversation. "You should be thankful Papi made you such a wonderful breakfast. It will give you

good energy for the day." She hugged her husband and gave him a kiss as she moved to serve a plate for him and one for herself. The two parents joined their children at the table and began to eat their breakfast tacos. The whining eventually died down and the children had to admit that if they were honest, they truly enjoyed the food.

Once they had finished eating, the children jumped up from the table and began to run away. "Don't forget to bring your plates over to the sink!" Mami reminded them. Once again, the complaining began.

"Why do I have to do EVERYTHING around here?!" moaned Rico.

"I hate having to clean up!" Diego mimicked his older brother.

After arguing with their parents for a few moments, the three kids eventually brought everything over to the sink, but by the time they were done, everyone was in a bad mood.

“Can we have a snack?” began Diego, his big brown eyes wide and begging as he gazed at his parents.

“You just ate breakfast, so no, you don’t need a snack,” said Papi firmly, shutting down the conversation before it could continue.

Before the kids could begin to whine again, Mami sent the three of them into the backyard to play as she worked to clean up the breakfast dishes and pots and pans. “If only these kids could appreciate

the many blessings that we have," she sighed.

Outside, Rico, Diego, and Araceli raced around on the grass, playing on the swingset, jumping on the trampoline, and kicking around a soccer ball. After about five minutes they ran out of steam.

"I'm bored! Why don't we have anything fun to do out here?" griped Rico.

Diego was quick to echo his older brother's sentiments. "There's nothing to do out here. I want to go inside and watch TV!"

Araceli watched her brothers and prepared to shout out the word "bored!" though she truly was having a great time and couldn't quite understand why her brothers were bored already. Then her face brightened as she looked past her brothers to the next yard. "Don Toño!" she squealed. She scrambled to run over to the chain-link fence that separated her yard from that of their neighbors, Don Toño and Doña Rosa.

The children loved their warm, friendly neighbors, and always ran to greet them when they saw them. They did their best to remember to address them with the polite terms "Don" and "Doña," which meant something like "Mr." and "Mrs."

Don Toño ambled over to the fence. *"¿Cómo estás, preciosa?"* he greeted Araceli in Spanish. "How are you, dear?"

"Bien," she answered with a shy smile on her face.

Diego and Rico ran over to the fence and said hello to their elderly neighbor. "*Hola*, Don Toño!" they said at the same time. The friendly Mexican man smiled back at his favorite young neighbors.

The relationship between the Martinez family and Don Toño and Doña Rosa was a special one. Papi and Mami had moved into the house when Rico was a baby. Doña Rosa had shown up at the door on move-in day with a covered plate full of Mexican *pan dulce*, or sweet bread. Papi was thrilled to see such a special treat that reminded him of

growing up in Mexico. The families made an instant connection.

Since that day, Papi had enjoyed sharing stories with his neighbors about his childhood in a Mexican city close to the town where Don Toño and Doña Rosa were from.

Doña Rosa had taken it upon herself to teach Mami to cook typical Mexican dishes for her family, since Mami had grown up in Minnesota eating traditional American foods. They had spent many happy afternoons in the kitchen together, cooking *enchiladas* and *pozole* and chatting in Spanish while the children played nearby.

Don Toño winked at the kids as he rested his arms on the fence. "I just came outside to water my garden, and I overheard some voices saying they were bored. How could that have happened so soon? Aren't you enjoying your summer vacation?" he asked.

"There's nothing to do here in this yard," said

Diego. "Summer is so boooooring!"

"Yeah, and we had a boring ol' breakfast of eggs and milk just like we do every day," added Rico. "Our life is so boring! I wish we could do something fun for a change."

"Boooriiiing!" repeated Araceli dramatically.

"Bueno," began the old man thoughtfully. "Today might be the day to introduce you to a special project I've been working on. Do you think you could keep busy for a few minutes while I speak with your parents?" The children nodded, and watched as he walked slowly to the front of the house to knock on the open screen door.

Chapter 2
The Door

After what seemed like forever, but was really only a few minutes, Don Toño returned to the backyard with Mami and Papi. "Your parents and I have agreed to let you kids help me test drive the new invention I've been working on. Would you be willing to help me out?"

Rico, Diego, and Araceli cheered. "Yay!" They followed their neighbor through the gate into his backyard. Don Toño led them over to the old garden shed located in the far corner of his property.

"Why are we going over to the shed? Do we have to help you do yard work?" asked Rico accusingly.

1 2 3
4 5 6
7 8 9
* 0 #

"That sounds even MORE boring!"

Don Toño turned around and raised a bushy gray eyebrow at Rico, then took hold of the shed door and opened it. The kids gasped in unison. Behind the ordinary shed door was a high-tech, metal door with a glowing keypad in the middle. Don Toño quickly punched in a long string of numbers, and the kids stared in astonishment as the door slid open. The interior of the shed was so dark that the children were not able to see anything inside.

"Mis amigos, this is not just a garden shed. It is a high-tech portal that uses virtual reality to transport its users to another land. I have been working on this project for years, but Doña Rosa and I are the only people who have tried it out. I think it's time we test it out with its intended audience: kids!"

Diego looked at it cautiously. "How does it work?"

Don Toño smiled kindly at Diego, then looked at Rico, Araceli, and their parents. "It is like walking

into a video game. You will be right here the whole time, but you will feel like you are moving around. How about we all go together for the first time?"

Mami and Papi glanced at each other, then nodded. "*Vámonos, pues!* Let's go!" Don Toño said happily and stepped through the shed door. Immediately he disappeared into the darkness.

Papi glanced at his wife, then pushed back his shoulders bravely and followed his neighbor into the shed. The kids heard him say, *"¡Órale!"* in excitement. "Come inside, *mi amor!*" he called to Mami, who was trying to see in from outside.

Mami looked back at her children, then took a deep breath and stepped into the dark shed. Her voice traveled out as if she were just a few feet away. "Oh my goodness! This is the coolest thing I've ever seen!" The kids tried to peer inside, but all they could see was darkness. "Come on in, kids!" their mother called. "We are right here. You are going to want to see this."

Rico and Diego stood frozen, looking at the open shed door. Araceli glanced at her older brothers, then at the door. "My turn!" she shouted, and took off running through the door. Instantly they heard her squeal in delight and begin to laugh happily.

"What is inside?" questioned Rico and Diego. They looked at the darkness, then at each other. "Let's go in together!" they decided. "One, two, three!" They grabbed hands and ran together into the shed, expecting to bump into their family and Don Toño in the darkness.

Unexpectedly, as they passed through the door, the darkness turned to light. They blinked and were surprised to find that they were surrounded by sunlight and green leaves. "What in the world?" murmured Rico. They had somehow been transported into a leafy forest!

"Woooah!" said both boys at the same time.

Chapter 3
Into the Trees

"Is that you, Rico? You look like a squirrel!" exclaimed Diego to his brother.

"So do you!" replied Rico to Diego. Looking down, the two brothers realized that they were actually balanced nimbly on a tree branch high above the ground, clutching it with their squirrel paws. Long, bushy tails waved behind them. "This is CRAZY!" said Rico. "I am a squirrel! How did Don Toño do this? And where is everyone else?"

At that moment, a small brown squirrel came scampering up. "Me squirrel!" exclaimed the energetic little creature. They recognized the voice as Araceli. She took off scampering on her four

feet and leaped from the branch she was on to a nearby tree branch. "So fun! Come!" she demanded of her brothers, who were still frozen in place. Araceli took another flying leap and scampered off through the treetops confidently.

"*¡Vamos, chicos!* Come on! It's just virtual reality! You can't get hurt!" called Don Toño's voice from up above them. Rico and Diego looked up to see a gray, grizzled, older-looking squirrel talking to them from a higher branch.

Just then, two larger squirrels scampered up, and from the way they were chattering excitedly in Spanish, the boys knew immediately that they were Mami and Papi. "Isn't this fun, kids? I could spend all day here playing in the treetops. We are lucky to have such a great neighbor, aren't we?" marveled Mami. "Oh, *amor,* I have to go finish painting the bedroom. Will you come with me?" she asked her husband.

Papi looked over at his squirrel wife and sighed. "I do have some work to do." He turned to the gray squirrel. "Don Toño, are you sure you are fine having the kids with you?"

"Of course! I love these *chamacos* like they were my own grandkids. You go get some work done. We'll be right here and the kids will be home in time for lunch." assured Don Toño. "You can go right out that hole over there to get out."

The two larger squirrels scampered over to a hollow in a tree trunk that the kids hadn't noticed until then. In a second they were gone. "*Amores*, be good for Don Toño, OK?" they heard their father's voice call from the hole.

"We promise!" the three little squirrels assured their parents in unison.

The three little squirrels scampered around from tree to tree, chasing each other through the branches in a game of tag like they had never played before. "This is so much more fun than our

house!" exclaimed Diego. Rico nodded his furry little head excitedly in agreement.

The squirrels scurried and raced through the trees, amazed with how easy it was to run up and down the tree trunks. After about twenty minutes, though, Rico stopped. "Don Toño, I'm hungry. Can we have a snack?"

"Yeah, I'm hungry after all this climbing," said Diego.

"Snack!" repeated Araceli. She ran over and lifted her little squirrel paws up as if she were begging for food.

Don Toño twitched his nose and waved his bushy tail. "Of course!" he said to them. Let me take you to my food stash." He led them up an oak tree trunk to another hollow. Poking his front half into the hollow so that only his bushy tail showed, he reached in, then popped back out. "Crunchy acorns for each of you!" he announced proudly, and handed each squirrel an acorn.

"Acorns?! Yuck! I don't eat acorns! I'm a kid!" responded Diego with a disgusted look on his furry little face.

Don Toño looked at the three little squirrels who were staring at the huge acorns in their paws. "Sorry kids, this is what you get when you're a squirrel. Eat it or wait til you get home for lunch." He settled back against the tree trunk and closed his eyes. "I'm going to take a short *siesta.* You little *ardillas* have fun!"

Chapter 4
Coco

Rico felt his stomach growling and he looked down at the acorn, still clutched between his two paws. He cautiously used his long front teeth to take a small nibble. He was surprised to find that it didn't taste as bad as he had imagined, and it had a nutty, crunchy texture. "I suppose that I can eat this for now, but it's not my favorite," commented Rico. Diego and Araceli followed his lead and tasted their acorns. They agreed with their brother. It wasn't great, but it was food.

"Wow, I'm glad I'm not a squirrel. I would have to eat this every day!" exclaimed Diego.

"You're right about that! I'm soooo bored of

eating acorns!" said an unfamiliar voice. The three squirrels turned around so quickly that their bushy tails brushed each other in the face as they looked to see where the voice was coming from. They were surprised to see a squirrel with glossy white fur posed gracefully on the branch next to them.

"I'm Coco! I live in that tree up there! Are you new to the forest?" Rico, Diego, and Araceli introduced themselves to the friendly squirrel, then Coco continued. "I don't know why anyone would want to come here. It's sooooo boring!"

Rico spoke up. "No it's not! It's fun to be a squirrel! You get to climb trees and jump on branches. Why would you say it's boring?"

"Yeah!" added Diego. "It feels like I'm flying when I run fast and jump so far."

Araceli smiled at Coco and tried to pet her fluffy white tail.

Coco giggled and twitched her tail. "That tickles!"

She looked at the three Martinez squirrels with a mischievous look on her face. "Does anyone want to play tag with me?" She took off with the three little squirrels chasing after her.

The friendly albino squirrel led them scampering through the forest. They chattered as only squirrels can as they scurried, climbed, and jumped through the leaves and branches. "I wish I could be a squirrel all the time! This is so much fun!" said Diego.

Coco looked at her new friends thoughtfully. "You know, you're right! It is pretty fun to be a squirrel. I guess because I do the same thing every day, it doesn't feel that fun to me anymore, and I probably take it for granted. I shouldn't, though. I really am glad I'm a squirrel. Thanks for reminding me!"

Rico's stomach growled again. "I wonder what Mami is making for lunch today? Do you think she's going to make *quesadillas* with crispy cheese?" His mouth began to water as he imagined his mother's specialty.

"What's a *quesadilla*?" asked Coco. "I eat acorns for breakfast, lunch, and dinner every day."

Rico and Diego described the spicy melted pepper jack cheese and sliced turkey folded into a warm corn tortilla to the albino squirrel, suddenly wishing they were home. Somehow Coco didn't seem quite as excited as they felt. "I think I might just stick to acorns for now," she responded.

The squirrels continued to play tag. Suddenly Coco stopped, and her cute little face scrunched up. "I'm bored. There's nothing to do around here but play tag. I wish we could do

something else."

Diego spoke up. "You should come over to our backyard someday. We have a trampoline that is really fun to jump on! And a swing set and a bunch of toys." He looked thoughtful. "I guess we do have a lot of cool things to do at home. I'm not quite sure how to get there from here, though."

At that moment the gray old squirrel they recognized as Don Toño came up. *"Niños,* your mami is calling you to go home for lunch. I think she mentioned you were going to have quesadillas today."

The Martinez squirrels began to whine about having to leave so soon, but their growling stomachs reminded them that they really wanted to eat something other than acorns for lunch. They looked sadly at their new friend Coco. "I hope we see you again," said Rico.

"Yes, play soon!" affirmed Araceli.

Don Toño spoke. "You can come back here another day. Just let me know and I will set up the virtual reality on the shed so you can come back. However, my little *ardillas*, it is time to go home now."

Coco gave each Martinez squirrel a warm squirrel hug, wrapping her beautiful white tail around each of her new friends. "Promise me you'll come back soon," she begged. "It's so much fun to have someone to play with."

The Martinez squirrels promised her they would be back. Then they followed Don Toño to the hollow in the oak tree that led them home. They were surprised that as soon as they scampered into the hole, they stepped out of the shed into the sunlight of Don Toño's backyard. Mami stood in front of them. "Did you have a fun time?" she asked them with a wink at Don Toño.

The three Martinez kids looked at each other, then down at themselves, briefly disappointed to be back in human form. Then Rico excitedly spoke up. "It was epic!" he shouted. "We might be the only

kids on earth who have experienced what it feels like to be a squirrel!"

Diego agreed. "I loved being a squirrel! You know, though, I think it might have gotten a little bit boring if I had to do it every day. All they do is eat acorns and run through the trees. I want to jump on the trampoline this afternoon!"

"Me too!" agreed Rico. "But first, let's go eat *quesadillas*! Mami, I love the food that you and Papi make for us to eat!"

"Yay! Eat!" agreed Araceli.

Rico looked at his neighbor, also back in human form. *"Gracias,* Don Toño! That was amazing!" Diego and Araceli also echoed their thanks, then turned to scamper after Mami to the house. All the while, the Martinez kids chattered about their adventure in the treetops and their new squirrel friend, Coco.

Don Toño waved at his neighbors as they headed

to their house next door. "*Hasta pronto, niños.* Wait til you see the other adventures I have planned for you." The wise old man walked over to his watering can, picked it up, and began to water his flowers.

High above his head, a little white squirrel scurried through the tree branches and scampered away.

Part 2

THE OCEAN ADVENTURE

Chapter 1
The Secret Mission

It was a rainy summer day, and the Martinez kids were busy coloring and drawing at the kitchen table. Araceli was coloring in her mermaid coloring book and occasionally decorating her hands and face with washable markers. Rico and Diego were working to draw an ocean scene on a big sheet of paper, illustrating vicious-looking sharks with long sharp teeth. They were excited to add more drawings to the gallery of pictures taped to the walls in their bedroom.

"You know what would make this picture even better?" suggested Rico. "If Mami would let us use her special colored pencils it would look so much more *chido.*"

Diego looked at him thoughtfully. "But she doesn't let us use them. She says they are just for her to use," he reminded Rico.

"Diego, go ask her if she will let us use them!" directed Rico. Diego started to disagree with his older brother, then changed his mind and obediently ran to the living room, where his mother was sitting and talking on her phone.

"Mami, can we use your special colored pencils?" he begged with his big brown eyes looking up at

her. Mami held up her hand to signal that she was listening to the person speaking to her.

"Just a second," she said into the phone. She looked at Diego. "No, Diego, you know that those are only for me to use. You have your own pencils and crayons to use."

"But Mami..." Diego began to whine. Mami put her finger up to shush him, then continued her phone conversation. Dejectedly, Diego hung his head and walked back to his brother at the table. "She said no," he stated sadly.

Rico looked at his brother and suddenly had an idea. "You know, Diego, I've seen where Mami keeps them. She isn't really paying attention right now. I bet we could grab them and take them downstairs and she wouldn't even know."

"But wouldn't we get in trouble?" asked Diego.

"Only if she catches you," said Rico with a gleam in his eye. "She keeps them in a drawer in her

room. If you walk casually past her while she's on the phone, she won't think anything of it. Tuck them under your shirt and take them down to the basement. I'll be waiting for you there."

"Why do I have to do it?" Diego looked frustrated. "I don't think this is a good idea."

"Come on! You're the little one. If you get caught you can just pout at her with your puppy dog eyes and she will forgive you. Go right now before she gets off the phone." Rico looked at Diego, knowing his brother would have a hard time standing up to him.

"OK...." agreed Diego reluctantly. He tiptoed cautiously in the direction of the living room.

"Don't be so obvious!" coached Rico, still seated safely at the kitchen table. Diego tried to look natural as he walked into the living room and began to move toward his parents' room.

His mother's voice interrupted him. "Diego, Rico,

Araceli, come here. I was just talking to Doña Rosa. She and Don Toño are going to take care of you today while Papi and I go to a meeting with the financial planner. Get your socks and shoes on. We're leaving in five minutes."

HARINA
de TRIGO
All-Purpose Flour

Chapter 2
Tortillas de Harina

Diego sighed in relief that his secret mission would have to wait. He obeyed his mother and put on his raincoat to run through the downpour to the house next door. Araceli trotted happily beside her mother, sticking her tongue out to catch the raindrops and not seeming to care at all about getting wet. Rico scowled grumpily as he followed behind, disappointed that his brother hadn't had a chance to snatch his mom's beautiful pencils. He briefly considered sneaking inside the house again to get them, but his father stepped out the door and locked it.

"Ándale, Rico. Move it. We're in a little bit of a rush here," he said to his son as he guided him to the neighbors' door.

Doña Rosa answered the door with a warm smile on her cheerful face. *"Buenos días, mi´jo.* Good morning, my boy. It is so good to see you on this rainy day."

Her silver hair was pulled up in a loose bun. She wore a blue and white apron embroidered with a bright Mexican pattern over her yellow blouse. "I was just about to make my famous *tortillas de harina.* Would you help me?"

Rico had to smile. Handmade flour tortillas were his neighbor's specialty. He joined his siblings at the sink to wash their hands, then settled at the table and waited for his turn to help Doña Rosa mash the flour mixture in a bowl with his hands. After that, she plopped a ball of dough in front of each child and handed them rolling pins. They worked to transform their balls of dough into flat tortillas. "Aww, why do mine always turn out looking like a map?" complained Rico as he looked at the jagged pattern he had formed.

"La práctica hace el maestro," she said wisely as

she easily created a perfect flattened circle on the table in front of her. "Practice makes perfect." Rico and Diego focused on their rolling pins, and Araceli played with her dough at the table. Doña Rosa stood up from the table and went to set the uncooked tortillas on the hot griddle known as a *comál.*

"Diego, you should have brought over Mami's colored pencils. We could have used them to work on our ocean picture," Rico whispered.

Diego looked at his brother bravely. "I don't want to take her pencils. You should have taken them if you wanted to use them so badly. But you didn't want to get in trouble, so you made me do it." He glanced up over Rico's head to see Don Toño watching from the doorway to the kitchen.

"Those tortillas smell *deliciosas*!" he announced to the group.

"Don Toño!" chorused the three children, who were starting to get tired of tortilla flattening. "Do

you have any new adventures in your magic shed for us to try out?" asked Diego. The three children turned to look at their neighbor pleadingly with their big, brown eyes.

The wise old man looked from the children to his wife who was still standing by the stove. *"Mi vida,* do you think you can spare your helpers for a little while? I do have a new project that I think would be perfect for today."

Doña Rosa smiled at her husband fondly. *"Claro que sí.* Of course," she said. "They have been such a big help today, but I can take care of it from here."

"Yaaaay!" cheered the children. They ran to wash their hands, then followed Don Toño to the door.

"Don't forget your raincoats. We don't want you to get wet," he reminded them as he led them out the back door of the house and toward the shed at the back of the yard. Opening the door, he punched in the long keycode and the high-tech door opened. The children stared into the darkness. "Remember,

it's just virtual reality. You'll be perfectly safe," he reminded the children.

"I'm not scared this time!" said Rico boldly. He looked at Diego and Araceli, then stepped forward into the darkness. Araceli and Diego followed close behind. As they passed through the door, they immediately felt different...and wet. Rather than standing in a stuffy shed, they were floating underwater!

Chapter 3
Swimming Lessons

"We're swimming! In the ocean!" bubbled Diego enthusiastically. He tried to look down at his body to figure out what kind of animal he was, but he wasn't able to bend his head to figure it out. "What am I?" he asked.

"Woooah! You're a killer whale!" said Rico to his brother as he examined the huge, shiny, black and white patterned body, tail, fins, and long black dorsal fin sticking straight up on his back.

A tiny seahorse swam up. "Many people prefer to call them orcas these days," said a familiar voice that the kids identified immediately. "Orcas eat marine animals like seals, but wild orcas have never hurt a human."

“Don Toño! You’re a seahorse! You’re so tiny, I can barely see you. But wait, if Diego is a killer whale, am I a whale too?” asked Rico.

“You are a whale shark,” answered Don Toño from his long, narrow seahorse snout as he swam back to look Rico’s body from head to tail, eyeing his wide mouth and the small white spots on his enormous black body.

"Cool, a shark! Does that mean I eat people?" considered Rico.

"Actually," corrected Don Toño, "Whale sharks aren't dangerous to humans. Even though you are 40 feet long and weigh 20 tons, you eat tiny little plankton that you filter from the water."

"Eewww!" said Rico. "That sounds kind of gross. I guess I'm glad I don't eat people though." He stopped to look through the crystal blue water. "Where is Araceli?" he asked.

Just then, a shiny, gray bottlenose dolphin swam quickly past them, moving upwards toward the shimmering surface of the water. She propelled herself so quickly with her strong tail and fins that she leaped out of the water, made a little flip and chirped adorably, then entered smoothly back into the ocean.

The dolphin swam up to the orca and whale shark. "Me dolphin! Jump!" They knew instantly it was Araceli.

"Araceli, that was a cool trick! How did you do that? You're only two!" said Diego.

Don Toño looked at them. "I think you'll be surprised at how powerful your instincts are. Try it out! Go for a swim in the Gulf of Mexico, *chicos*... I mean, flippered friends."

Diego gave a flip of his tail and flippers and discovered that his orca body did know how to swim, and fast. He made his own leap out of the water, admiring the blue sky and how the turquoise sea sparkled below him, then gracefully reentered the water. "Try it, Rico!" Diego shouted to his brother.

Rico prepared to propel himself into a leap with his tail and fins, but was disappointed to discover that he could not pick up enough speed to leap into the warm, tropical sunshine. "Aw, what happened?" he asked.

"Oh, I forgot to tell you that whale sharks aren't able to leap out of the water," apologized Don Toño. Rico watched helplessly as his brother and sister continued to leap and play near the surface of the water, and decided to suggest a game he could play too.

Chapter 4
The Undersea Heist

"Catch me, slowpokes!" called Rico the whale shark. He took off swimming, deeper and deeper, and discovered that the water started to get darker and colder. The surface looked farther away than he remembered. Rico tried to turn his head to look for his siblings behind him, but remembered too late that he didn't have a neck. He moved clumsily to turn his enormous body around, and was surprised to bump into a strange-looking creature much smaller than himself, with eight long tentacles covered in suction cups.

"Hey, watch where you're going!" said the octopus to Rico. "Smaller sea creatures should have the right of way. Be careful."

Rico stammered. "I'm so very sorry, Mr. Octopus. I am still learning how to move around."

"You can call me Octavio," said the octopus slickly as he saluted with one of his flowing tentacles. "I haven't seen you around these parts. Are you new to the area? I think it would be kind of hard to miss the biggest fish in the sea swimming around."

Rico smiled a wide smile, showing his teeny-tiny teeth. "Yes, I'm new here. Can you help me? I lost my brother and sister."

Octavio blinked his enormous eyes and stared at Rico. "There are two more of you?"

"Well, actually, they look a little different from me… never mind," answered Rico weakly, asking himself how he would ever explain his situation to his new eight-limbed friend. "On second thought,

how about you just show me around?"

Octavio nodded his giant head and gestured with a tentacle covered in suction cups. "Actually, I was just on my way to take care of something. I think you could be helpful."

"Sure!" responded Rico happily. "How can I help you?"

"I need you to distract the other sea creatures for a minute. Can you do that? Just swim over in that direction, down near the ocean floor. We haven't seen a whale shark around here for a while, so everybody will be excited to see you. Then meet me back here in about eight minutes," he finished, showing all eight tentacles.

Rico looked at Octavio. He wasn't really sure what was going on, but it was part of the adventure, right? He took off swimming in the direction that the octopus had pointed. As he swam, he admired the colorful clownfish, angelfish, starfish, and other tiny sea creatures who all turned to stare at him as he moved gracefully by. "Hello, fishies!"

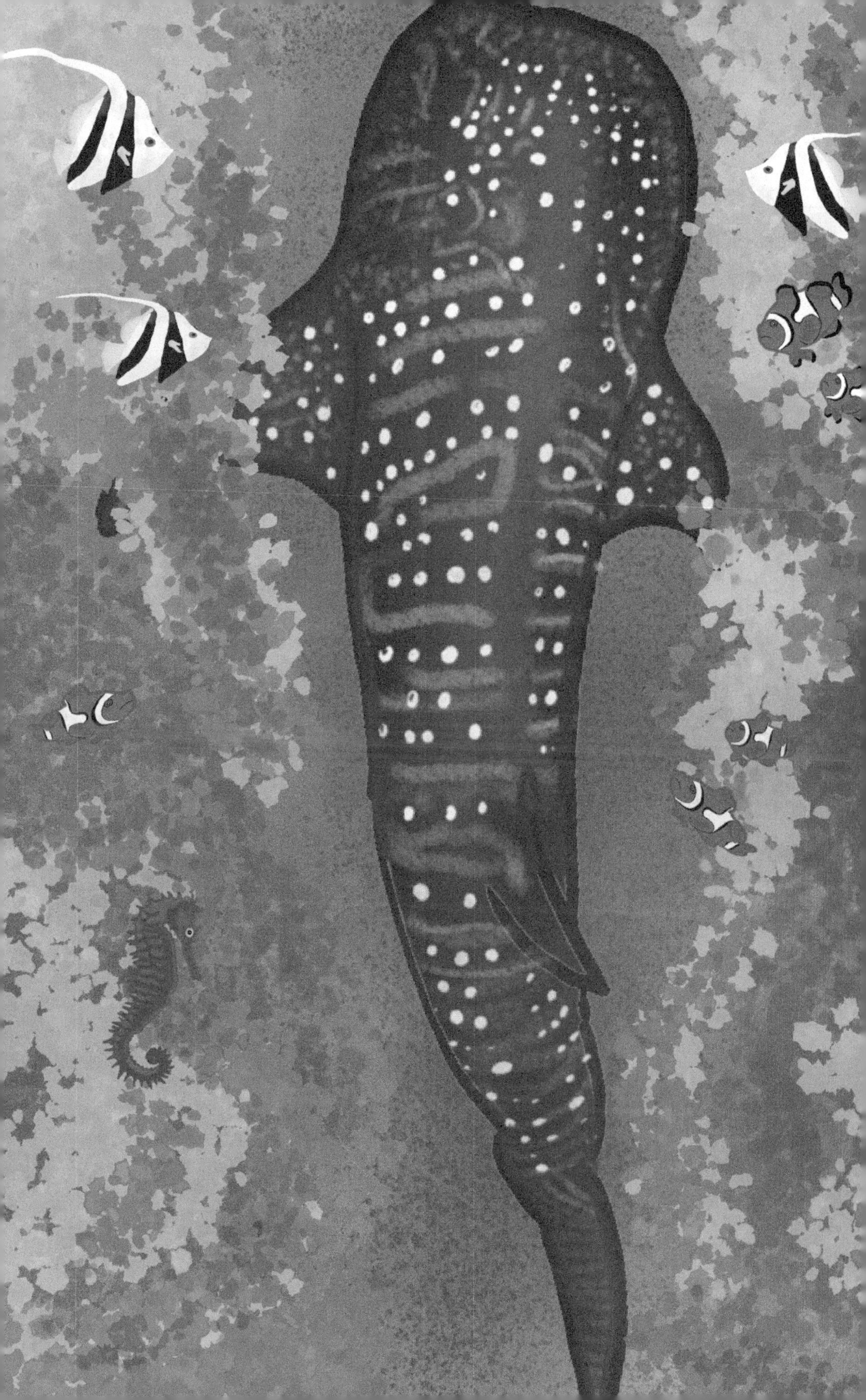

he said, trying to wave with his giant flipper and accidentally creating a current that swept some of the creatures away from him. "Oops, sorry!" he apologized.

Rico enjoyed his sudden fame, swimming past the sea animals and smiling and waving like he was on a parade float. Suddenly he realized he had lost his way. He turned to swim through a colorful coral reef as he looked for Octavio. And then he saw him.

Octavio the octopus drifted toward a hollow in the coral reef. He changed color, camouflaging himself to blend into the coral around him. Making his body long and skinny, he inserted one tentacle into the hole and pushed it through. He continued to slide through the hole, one tentacle at a time. Finally, he squeezed his large head through the tiny opening in the coral and disappeared.

Rico moved closer to peer through the hole. What he saw inside made him gasp.

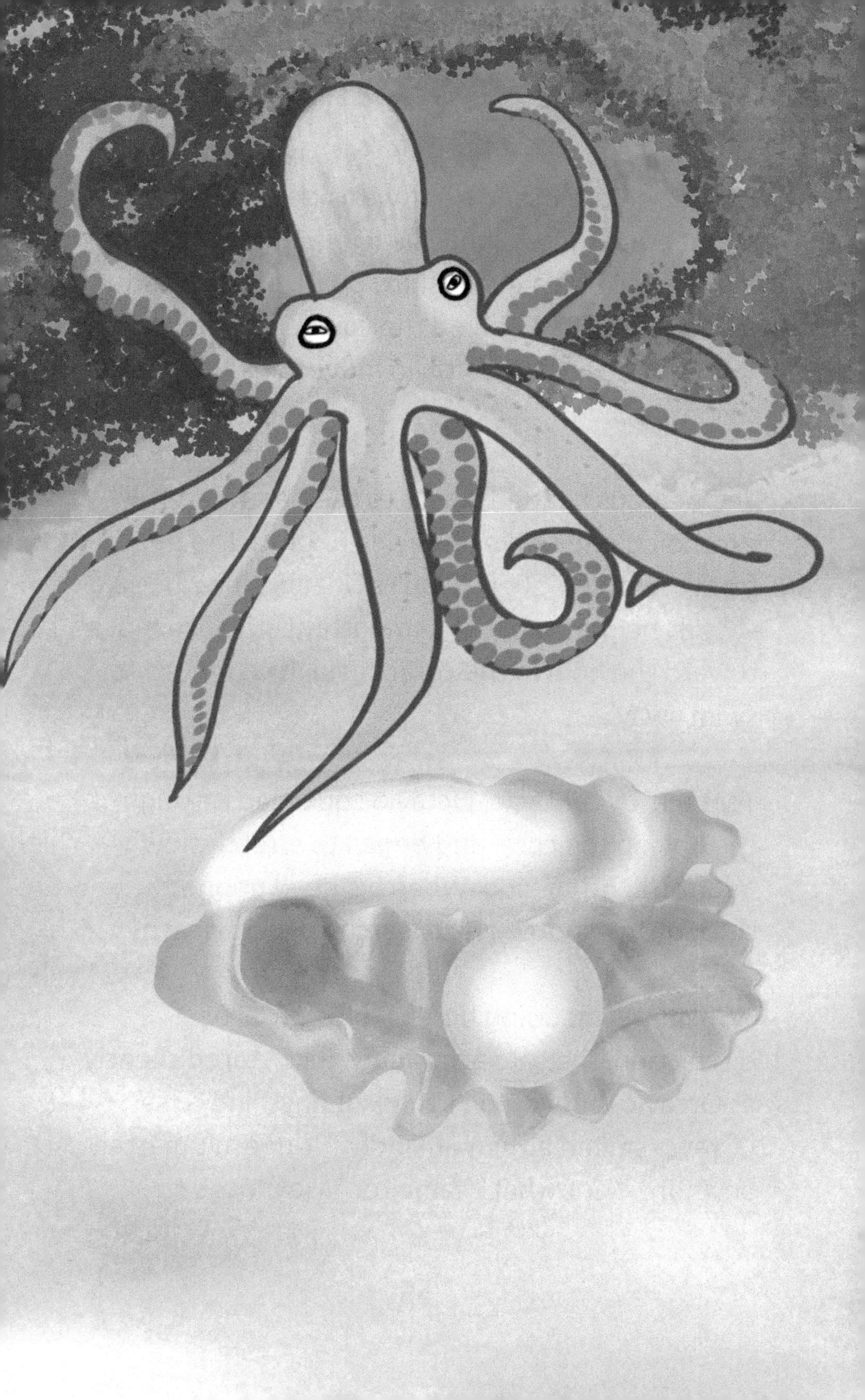

Resting on the ocean floor was a beautiful, shimmering oyster shell. Sitting in the middle of the shell was a giant, shiny pearl. Rico gulped nervously. He hid behind the coral and watched through the hole as Octavio moved ahead on his secret mission.

The octopus headed closer to the pearl, carefully extending one of his tentacles to pluck the pearl from the oyster shell. "You're finally mine," he said slyly as he grasped it. He smoothly turned to move toward the hole in the coral again. Rico moved to swim away.

Tentacle by tentacle, Octavio squeezed through the hole in the coral and began to stretch slowly out of the other side. When his head popped through, he spotted Rico watching from nearby.

"What are you doing here? I told you to be a distraction," he said accusingly. Rico stared silently at Octavio, but couldn't think of anything to say. Octavio smiled at him unkindly. "It doesn't matter anymore. I got what I came for." He moved to

pull his final tentacle out through the hole, but it stopped suddenly. He tugged and grunted. "I'm stuck! The pearl is too big to fit through the hole!" he said in a frustrated voice. "What am I going to do now?" he grumbled to himself.

Rico looked at the eight-tentacled thief, took a deep breath through his gills, then stuttered out his answer. "That pearl isn't yours, is it? Why did you take it?"

Octavio, still with one tentacle stuck in the hole in the coral, looked at Rico. "It's mine now! That oyster can make another one whenever it wants." He yanked his trapped tentacle again, but was unable to pull it through with the giant pearl clutched on the inside. "Help me out, will you?" he said to Rico helplessly.

Rico looked at Octavio, then bravely responded. "I think you should put it back. You shouldn't take things that aren't yours. That's stealing. You'll feel better about yourself if you are honest. Even if nobody catches you, it's wrong to take something that isn't yours."

Octavio gazed silently back at him and tried once more to pull the pearl through the hole.

Rico tried to shrug, amused to remember he had no shoulders. "It's up to you to do the right thing, Octavio. I wish I had never helped you out. You were never a real friend to me. Goodbye now."

He turned a wide circle to swim away from Octavio the octopus, who was still trapped with one tentacle in the hole, clutching the pearl tightly. "Come back, whale shark! Help me!" he shouted as Rico swam away and up towards the surface of the water.

Chapter 5
The Pearl

Rico found Diego the orca and Araceli the dolphin playing happily together, swimming in circles and leaping acrobatically out of the water with artistic spins. Don Toño the seahorse swam quickly up to him. "Where were you, Rico? We couldn't find you. Your *hermano y hermana* wanted to play some water games with you." He gazed wisely at Rico. "Or maybe you had something more important to get out of this time under the sea. *¿Es cierto?*"

The large spotted whale shark looked at the wise seahorse. "Yeah, I did learn something." He turned to Diego, who had swum up nearby. "You were right, Diego. It's wrong to take things that don't belong to us. I'm sorry for trying to make you take

Mami's colored pencils today."

Diego the black and white orca looked at Rico the whale shark. "That's OK," he forgave his brother quickly. "Hey, do you want to have a swimming competition with Araceli and me? She's a lot smaller than us but she's pretty good at tricks."

Rico looked at Diego and Araceli, then over at Don Toño. "Sure, let's do it! Have you seen my underwater spin? I'm going to out-swim both of you!"

Diego and Araceli laughed as they watched Rico attempt to rotate underwater as he moved his enormous body slowly forward.

Don Toño the seahorse floated over to the trio. "We might need to work on those tricks another day. Doña Rosa is waiting for us with lunch. She promised she was going to make *chiles rellenos* today."

"Stuffed peppers? That sounds so much better than plankton," said Rico. The whale shark, orca, and dolphin swam behind the seahorse toward a big

hole in the coral. As soon as they passed through, they found themselves back on solid land.

"It may take a little while to get used to your land legs again," chuckled Don Toño as he saw the three children flopping on their bellies on the green grass outside the shed.

He reached down to help each of them up, and the friends walked on wobbly legs to the house where Doña Rosa was waiting with a delicious-smelling lunch set out on the table. *"A comer,* time to eat," she said as she smiled warmly at her favorite neighbor children.

As he walked into the dining room, Rico's heart stopped and his eyes widened. A framed photo of a much younger Doña Rosa in a wedding dress was mounted on the wall. Dangling from a necklace around her neck was a large, beautiful, shiny pearl. "Doña Rosa, where did you get that pearl?" he asked her breathlessly.

Doña Rosa looked over at Don Toño and a wistful look came over her face. "That *perla* was a special gift given to me by *mi amor* on our wedding day. A few weeks ago my necklace fell off as I was doing some yard work. When I went back to look for it later it was gone. Somebody must have seen it and taken it." She paused as a tear glistened in her eye. "It was irreplaceable!"

Rico's heart felt heavy as he watched his kind-hearted neighbor's sad face. He wondered who would be so mean as to steal an old lady's necklace. He tried to enjoy the *chiles rellenos* but even his favorite food did not taste as good as he remembered.

Just then, the doorbell rang. *"Ya voy!* I'm coming!" called Doña Rosa as she walked to open the front door. "Hello? Who's there?" she called. As his neighbor was about to close the door, Rico spotted a small cardboard box sitting on the front step. He ran to pick it up and handed it to Doña Rosa.

Doña Rosa brought the box inside and set it on the table. “What could this be?” she asked herself as she opened the box. She unfolded a piece of paper and read aloud:

I TOOK SOMETHING
THAT WASN'T MINE
AND I FEEL SO GUILTY.
PLEASE FORGIVE ME.

Then Doña Rosa reached into the box and unwrapped a small cloth. She gasped and tears sprang to her eyes. She began to sob and laugh at the same time. The children ran to see what she was looking at. Nestled in the cloth at the bottom of the box lay Doña Rosa's beautiful pearl necklace.

Part 3

THE RAINFOREST ADVENTURE

Chapter 1
The Dare

It was a beautiful summer morning, and the Martinez kids were out playing in the backyard. The sun was shining, and a gentle breeze blew the green leaves of the trees that shaded the swing set. Rico, Diego, and Araceli were pretending they were ninja warriors, hanging, swinging, and climbing as they completed their routine.

"I wonder if we can go to the ninja park this afternoon?" wondered Diego. "This is getting too easy!"

"Yeah!" agreed Rico. "We're getting to be really amazing climbers!"

Behind them, they heard their sister's voice. "Me monkey!" she said. They turned around and laughed as they saw her hanging by her arms from the top post of the swingset.

"Araceli, be careful," said Diego as he went to help her down. "You might think you're a monkey, but you're just a little girl."

His little sister studied him for a minute, then turned around and started climbing up the slide. Diego considered reminding her that she needed to climb up the ladder to slide down, but he was distracted by his brother's voice.

"Look, Diego! I bet you can't do this!" Rico had shimmied up the swing set support and was lying on his belly on the top post, clutching it with his arms and legs.

Diego looked up at his brother. "You're a lot bigger than I am. I don't think it would be very safe for me to try that." He moved to sit down on the swing.

From up above, Rico called down. "Don't be a scaredy-cat, Diego. You're just a little baby," he taunted.

"I am not!" Diego shouted back up. He went over to the support post and tried to find a way to climb up to where his brother was perched. From up above, Rico laughed at his brother, and not in a kind way. "You're so little!"

Diego made his way to the top of the swingset and tried to grip the post with his body as he had seen his brother do. Suddenly, Diego lost his grip and slipped so that he was hanging upside-down by his arms and legs. He screamed. "Aaaah! Get Papi!"

Rico swung down quickly and went running to the door just as Papi came hurrying out after hearing his son's screams. He dashed over to the swingset and reached up his strong arms to rescue his son and set him on solid ground.

"¿Qué onda contigo?" he asked his younger son angrily after he had hugged him. "What were you thinking? Are you trying to get yourself killed?"

Diego hung his head. "Rico called me a baby scaredy-cat. I'm not!"

Papi looked at his sons. "Dieguito, *hijo,* you do not want to spend your summer with your leg in a cast or a head injury. Please do not take heedless risks. Rico, do not provoke your brother that way. You know he's smaller than you."

"Yes, Papi," mumbled Rico, looking down at the ground. He quickly changed the subject. "Hey, Papi, can we go to the ninja park in the afternoon?"

"That depends. Are you going to start making wise choices?" he asked them seriously.

"We'll be careful, Papi!" promised the boys.

Chapter 2
The Ninja Park

After lunch, the Martinez family drove in the van to the boys' favorite playground, which they called the "ninja park" because of all of the structures for climbing, swinging, and balancing. Rico, Diego, and Araceli took off excitedly, running in three different directions. Mami followed Araceli in the direction of the swings. Papi stood where he could see both Diego and Rico as they energetically balanced, climbed, and swung across the monkey bars.

Papi glanced down as a small child ran by him, screaming, with her mother chasing behind her. When he looked up, he realized he had no idea where his boys were. "They're old enough to play on their own," he told himself, and sat down on a bench to wait for his sons to appear again.

Up above on the playground, Rico climbed higher and higher on the cargo nets and ladders, moving from platform to platform. He came to the top of the large structure and glanced down to see Papi far below, sitting on a bench. He could see Araceli swinging with Mami on the other side of the park. Just as he was looking around for Diego, he heard a voice behind him. He swung around.

“Hey, kid. What’s your name?” asked a boy who was probably 10 or 11 years old. He had a stylish, spiky hairstyle and was smiling at Rico.

“Rico,” he responded quickly, excited to be getting attention from an older boy.

“I bet you can’t climb down on the top of the tube slide,” challenged the boy. He pointed to the slide that spiraled down past five levels of platforms on the way to the ground.

Rico’s eyes followed the slide to the bottom. “That doesn’t look very safe,” he said cautiously.

“Come on! All of the big kids do it. I guess you’re just too little and scared.” The boy paused dramatically. “That’s OK. I’ll go play with my other friends who are brave.” He turned to leave.

“Wait!” Rico said urgently. “I can do it!” He nervously started to climb over the barrier that protected children from falling 30 feet to the ground. He extended his foot and prepared to

stretch his leg to step onto the top of the tube slide.

"Rico, stop! What are you doing?!" Diego's urgent voice behind him caused him to halt. He turned his head to look at his younger brother. "Go away, Diego. I'm playing with the big kids now. Right…?"

He realized he didn't know the older boy's name as he gestured toward where he had been standing. He caught a glimpse of the spiky hair disappearing into the tube slide as the challenger made a quick getaway.

Rico sighed in relief. He didn't want anyone thinking he was a baby, but he really didn't want to fall to his death below him. He moved back down onto the platform. "Come on, Diego." He and his brother played happily on the ninja playground, climbing and swinging confidently across the monkey bars.

Later, as the family was heading home in the van, Diego spoke up. "Rico was showing off for a big kid

today and almost did something really dangerous." Rico glared at his brother.

Mami turned to look back at Rico from the passenger seat. "Is that true, Rico?" she asked.

Rico stared straight ahead as his parents lectured him on the importance of safety and thinking for himself. "Blah, blah, blah. It really wasn't a big deal," he mumbled to himself as he tuned his parents out.

When they reached the house, Mami took a sleeping Araceli inside to set her down for her nap. Papi headed to the deck to fire up the grill.

"Can we watch TV?" asked Diego and Rico in unison.

"No," responded Papi firmly. "I want you to play outside while I am grilling the *carne asada*. I'll let you know when it's time to eat dinner."

Just then, Don Toño stepped out from his house

and walked up to the boys. *"Buenas tardes, amiguitos,"* he greeted his friends. "Do you have time to try out my new project?" He looked at their father for approval.

"Please, Papi?" the boys begged, looking at their father with their famous puppy dog eyes.

"Ándale, pues," he said to them. "Go ahead, but when it's time to eat, I'll expect you to come back right away."

The boys agreed and raced through the gate into Don Toño's yard and toward the secret shed. "Hold on, boys! You can't go in until I start up the program." It seemed like it took forever for him to amble to the shed door and punch in the code. As soon as the fancy door opened, the boys looked at Don Toño. "Go ahead! I'll let you know when your Papi calls you for dinner."

The boys ran eagerly through the door, excited to see what their transformation would be this time.

Instantly the air felt heavy and damp. They were surrounded by leafy trees. Screeches of birds and buzzing of insects filled the air. Diego and Rico looked at each other in disbelief. “We’re in the jungle!” they yelled together.

Chapter 3
Rainforest Antics

"You're a monkey!" screamed Diego with delight. He reached out a long black furry arm to examine it, then patted his shaggy potbelly. "Am I a monkey too?"

"Yes, we're both monkeys! Now we are going to be the best ninja warriors ever!" exclaimed Rico exuberantly. "I dare you to climb to the very top of the tree!" he challenged Diego.

Diego looked at Rico sternly. "I thought Papi said not to do that anymore," he reminded him.

"We can't get hurt here. It's not even real!" said Rico. "Do it!" He gestured to the top of the largest tree they could see near them.

"¡Hola!" squawked a red macaw as it flew up to them and settled on the branch. "Looking good, my little spider monkeys!" It was Don Toño, in the form of a brilliantly-colored red parrot with bright blue, green, and yellow wings. "He's right, you know. You won't get hurt, but it might give you a bit of a scare if you fall, and then I'd have to restart the program. I wouldn't recommend throwing yourself to the ground to see what happens, but feel free to move around without fear."

The wise old bird looked past the curved point of his beak and rotated his head to see each of the boys out of the side of his head. "I figured you boys might want to experience life as spider monkeys. After watching your acrobatics in the yard, I could tell you like to climb. Now, go and explore the Mexican rainforest."

Diego batted away a large, colorful bug that buzzed past him. *"Gracias,* Don Toño," he said, and Rico echoed his thanks. Don Toño the macaw made a sound like a fire siren and flapped into the air, whistling shrilly. "He's going to scare the other

parrots," laughed Diego as they watched their friend fly away.

The two spider monkeys excitedly grabbed hold of the tree branch with their hook-like four-fingered hands, attempting to swing from one tree to the next. "This is kind of tricky," commented Rico as both boys practiced moving from branch to branch, using their arms as if they were playing on playground monkey bars.

Suddenly a black spider monkey about their size dropped down next to them, hanging from the branch above by his long tail and looking almost like a spider hanging from a thread. "That's because you're doing it wrong!" He landed lightly on the branch next to them. "I'm Yoyo!" he said with a mischievous smile on his friendly face. His beady black eyes peered at Diego and Rico. "You look like spider monkeys. But you don't move like spider monkeys. Did you forget how?"

The two glanced at each other. "Kind of," they admitted together. "Can you show us?" asked Diego.

"Sure!" affirmed Yoyo. "We may only have thumbs on our feet, but our tails are as good as another arm or leg."

He demonstrated how he was able to swing using his hands, feet, and even his tail, allowing him to move almost effortlessly through the rainforest canopy, high above the ground. After a bit of practice, Rico and Diego's spider monkey instincts kicked in, and they realized they were naturals.

"Tag! You're it!" shouted Yoyo. He reached out and tapped Diego on the furry arm. He took off swinging with Diego and Rico following him gleefully, swinging acrobatically through the trees by their five limbs.

Chapter 4
The Jungle Castle

Suddenly the boys noticed that the rainforest looked a little different. They were standing next to an old-looking concrete structure. "Where are we?" wondered the boys.

"This is *Las Pozas*," said Yoyo. "You have to check out the jungle castle when you come to Xilitla." Rico and Diego's mouths dropped open as they stepped from the jungle into a clearing. Rising up in the middle of the rainforest was what appeared to be an old, half-constructed castle with winding concrete staircases and wide columns supporting more platforms. High concrete arches shot up into the air with no apparent purpose.

"This is so much cooler than the ninja playground!" exclaimed Diego. The three spider monkeys swung from one level to the next, stretching out their long legs, arms, and tails as they climbed up the concrete structure.

"Hey, Yoyo, who are your friends? I bet *they* can jump all the way to the bottom from here," came a voice from behind the boys. Suddenly a bigger spider monkey with a spiky mohawk at the top of his furry head swung down and hung in front of them, blocking their way. "All of the brave spider monkeys do it."

Yoyo suddenly looked less confident as he looked back at the bigger monkey. "Uh, hi Bobo. I told you before, I don't think that would be very safe. The concrete is really hard and it's a really long way down."

The mohawked monkey looked back at Yoyo. "What are you scared of? Are you a little infant monkey? I bet you would feel better if your mom would let you ride on her back. You could wrap

your tail around hers like a seatbelt so you don't fall and get hurt. You're such a scaredy-monkey."

Yoyo looked very uncomfortable as Bobo continued to tease him. "I'm not an infant, and I'm not scared!" he said, though the boys weren't sure if he really believed it himself.

"Then prove it," urged the larger monkey. "Jump from the top of the castle to the ground. If you dare." He gazed at Yoyo with a smile that looked more like a sneer. "If you don't jump, I'll tell all the other spider monkeys you're an infant, and nobody will want to play with you."

Yoyo's face looked worried as he glanced at Rico and Diego, then began to nervously climb to the top of the structure. The two brothers stood frozen as they watched their new friend prepare to dive to the ground. Diego glanced at Bobo, who sat on the concrete platform watching Yoyo climb and laughing to himself.

Suddenly Diego yelled, "Yoyo! Don't jump! I

know you're not a baby! You don't need to prove yourself to Bobo the Bully." Yoyo paused in his climb to look at them while Bobo turned around to glare at Diego.

Rico piped in. "You're not a scaredy-monkey at all! You're really brave, and you taught us to do so many tricks. If you jump you could get hurt. Come back down and play with us, please."

Bobo looked like he was about to speak up again. Just then an even larger spider monkey came up. "Bobo, are you tormenting the smaller monkeys again? Wait til I tell your mother. Home. Now!" Bobo's father tugged Bobo's tail and the bully took off, reluctantly following his father through the rainforest.

Yoyo climbed back down to where Diego and Rico were resting on the castle structure. "What was I thinking?" he asked. "I just let Bobo get to me sometimes. He makes me feel like I have to prove myself to him."

Rico looked at Diego, then back at Yoyo. "You don't have to prove yourself to anybody. I bet Bobo would never do something that dangerous."

"Besides," added Diego, "You're the bravest monkey I know!"

Yoyo looked at his new friends thoughtfully. "Thanks, you guys. You two are true friends. Bobo has never been nice to me. Thanks for saving me from making a big mistake!" The three spider monkeys gave each other a group hug, wrapping their long tails together like it was a secret handshake. "Friends forever!" they promised.

Just then a red macaw came flying up to them. "Ah, I see that you've discovered Edward James' surrealist garden structure," Don Toño squawked as if he were their tour guide.

"What does that mean?" asked Diego.

"A rich artist made this castle weird like this on purpose so it would look *chido*," translated Rico.

The red macaw gave a screechy parrot laugh. *"Muy bien,* Rico," he affirmed. "Well, boys, I hate to do this to you, but your Papi let me know that it's time for dinner. The *carne asada* smells incredible. You'd better get home before all of the tacos are gone."

Yoyo blinked at them. "I have to find my own fruit and bugs for my dinner. Whatever your father is giving you sounds so much better than my food. Can I join you?"

Rico and Diego looked at Don Toño the macaw pleadingly. He fluttered his colorful wings and looked back at them, then at Yoyo. "Sorry, *muchacho.* Maybe another time. Thanks for showing these monkeys the ropes." Yoyo looked disappointed but said goodbye to Rico and Diego and took off into the rainforest.

The spider monkeys followed the macaw to a hole in a large tree and stepped inside. Transformed back into their human form, they stepped out of the shed into Don Toño's yard. Instantly, they smelled the delicious scent of grilled meat wafting

from Papi's grill next door. They thanked Don Toño and headed home.

As they walked into their yard and up the wooden steps to the deck, Rico spoke to Diego. "I dare you to climb up on top of the guardrail of the deck like a monkey. If you can't, you're a baby," challenged Rico.

Diego looked back at his brother. "I probably could, but I could fall and hurt myself. I don't have to prove myself to you or anybody," he responded firmly.

Rico sighed. "You're right," he said thoughtfully. "You know, Yoyo taught us a lot today. I loved being able to climb up to the top of the trees and swing around."

"Me too!" agreed Diego. "I wouldn't want to be a monkey all the time, but I sure am going to miss my tail!"

Chapter 5
Carne Asada

Rico and Diego climbed the wooden stairs to the deck, where Papi was removing steaming meat from the grill and placing it in a glass container. *"Hola, hijos,"* he greeted them with a smile. "I've invited Doña Rosa and Don Toño to join us for dinner."

"Yay!" celebrated the boys.

Araceli stepped out of the door from the house, her hair tousled after her nap. "Me help!" she said. She carried a handful of napkins to the picnic table and began to lay them out on the table, then squealed and scurried to run after them as a gust of wind blew them off. Rico moved to help her pick

them up, then placed a bowl on top of the pile so they wouldn't blow away again.

At that point, Araceli's eyes glanced up and her face brightened. "Hi!" she yelled as she spotted Doña Rosa and Don Toño walking through the gate.

Mami came out of the house carrying a stack of steaming tortillas wrapped in a cloth. In her other hand she carried a bowl of chopped onions, which she set down on the table. *"Bienvenidos!"* she said to her neighbors, who were climbing slowly up the wooden staircase to the deck. The elderly couple settled at the table and smiled fondly as the kids ran to sit by them, chattering excitedly at the same time.

When dinner was finally ready, the children began to devour their tacos, and their taste buds danced with the flavors of the corn tortillas filled with savory, thin-sliced beef, chopped onions, cilantro, salsa, and a squeeze of lemon.

At first, the children ate quietly as their parents conversed with their neighbors. A couple of tacos later, Rico spoke up. "Don Toño, do you think you could make an adventure about komodo dragons? They're my favorite reptile."

"Yeah!" agreed Diego. "Or maybe we could be real dragons… or dinosaurs!"

"Me koala!" added Araceli. "Me horsey! No, me unicorn!"

"Ooh! It would be really fun to fly! Could you make me an eagle?" suggested Rico.

"What about a jaguar? They're really scary!" suggested Diego.

Mami glanced at Papi, then spoke up. "Kids, please, give Don Toño a chance to breathe. He has already done so much for you." She turned to the kind man. *"Muchas gracias,"* she thanked him. "The kids can't stop talking about the magic door and their animal adventures."

Don Toño's eyes twinkled as he looked around the table at his favorite neighbor family. *"Es un placer,"* he said. "It's my pleasure to spend time with these *chamacos.* They keep me feeling young. Also, I appreciate the suggestions. I'm always looking for new ideas."

"Doña Rosa, when are YOU going to come on an adventure with us?" asked Diego.

The woman smiled. "I HAVE always wondered what it would feel like to be a hummingbird. *Mi amor*, do you think you could make that happen?"

Don Toño gazed lovingly at his wife. "Anything for you, my little *colibrí.*"

Papi looked mischievous. "I wonder if you could make me into a *chupacabras*?" he joked, referring to the urban legend about a made-up Mexican animal.

Mami elbowed her husband with a smile. "It might be kind of hard to turn you into a mythical animal.

You know, though, I have always thought it would be fun to be able to leap like a kangaroo."

Don Toño chuckled. "You're giving me a lot of work to do, but that's *fabuloso*! I love tinkering in my shed on new projects. I'll keep making them as long as you kids keep coming."

"And I'll keep making special Mexican treats to fuel your adventures," added Doña Rosa.

"You two are the best neighbors ever!" shouted Rico.

"¡Te amo!" said Araceli, giving Doña Rosa a tiny kiss on the cheek.

"We are the luckiest kids in the world!" exclaimed Diego.

Doña Rosa looked at Araceli, Diego, Rico, and their parents. "I'd say a better word is *bendecidos.* We are all blessed to be neighbors."

Everybody agreed, and the two families sat on the deck sharing stories, telling jokes, and laughing happily, until the sun set. 🌅

Please go to
www.mindagomez.com
to download a discussion guide for parents and children.

Contact Minda at:
martinezkidsadventures@gmail.com

Mami's Spicy Turkey Quesadillas

Ingredients:

1 Corn tortilla

2 Small slices of pepper jack cheese

1 Slice of deli turkey

Note: Mami reminds you to ask an adult for help when working with a hot stove and sharp knives.

nstructions:

1. Heat the griddle on the stove at medium temperature.
2. Cut two small slices of pepper jack cheese (about 1x2 inches).
3. Put your tortilla on the griddle and let it heat up for about 30 seconds.
4. Flip the tortilla over and place a slice of turkey on the tortilla.
5. Add the two slices of cheese on top of the turkey and fold the tortilla in half.
6. As the cheese begins to melt, press down with a spatula so that it oozes out and begins to get crunchy.
7. Flip the quesadilla over to cook on the other side.
8. Enjoy your quesadilla while it is still hot. Yum!

About the Author

Minda Gomez lives in Minnesota with her husband Moisés and their spunky bilingual kids named Rafa, Dante, and Amalia. Their family has created their own brand of "Mexigringo" as they blend their Papi's Mexican culture with their Mami's Minnesotan culture.

Minda is a teacher of English Learners at a local elementary school. She has taught second grade in Mexico and volunteered in Guatemala, Peru, and other parts of Latin America.

Minda is passionate about teaching children to be proud of their bilingual superpowers. She is hopeful that her readers and her own kids will identify with the Martinez family, and remember that speaking more than one language is one of the many things that can make a kid special.

Made in the USA
Columbia, SC
28 March 2022